How to Train Your Ender Dragon 3–
Separated!

Funny Comics

Special Bonus

Be sure to read to the back of the book for information on how to get FREE Kindle comics, including our very first comic "The Jousting Tournament", from Funny Comics!

Be sure to "LIKE" our Funny Comics Facebook Page by clicking below

https://www.facebook.com/FunnyComics3000

Subscribe to Funny Comic's YouTube channel here

Funny Comics YouTube Channel

https://www.youtube.com/channel/UC61rZRtwDl79igc5ltb1Hcg/videos

Be sure to watch our epic Star Wars / Minecraft Mashup "Attack On The Death Square!"

Other Books In This Series

Chapter 1 – Prelude to a Storm

OH MY *GOD*.

I am going to start crying and bawling any moment now. I am not even exaggerating – I have actual tears in my eyes.

Mavrose is missing.

My beautiful, fierce and absolutely powerful Ender Dragon is *missing*.

And the worst of it is – I cannot even feel her mind any more!

For a Dragon Rider, it is the worst thing to experience, to have your dragon's mind torn away from yours. Once you get used to having the constant presence of your dragon at the back of your head, the sudden silence is almost painful.

Mavrose is *missing*.

She's gone, and I cannot feel her. Oh god, I can't breathe, I can't do anything right now! I need to pull myself together and I need to go find her! I need... I need my dragon back!

Who knows what kind of torture she is going through? Who knows where she is? I haven't seen her in almost an entire week! I don't know if she ate, if she is tied up or if she is hurt in any way! The last glimpse I had of her was when she was roaring into the fire and jumping in to save Baya. Baya made it out, but she has been with the Healers since then and Mavrose has not been seen since!

I don't even know if she is alive. The Shahleigh informed me that if she *were* dead, then my instinctive bond with her would let me know, even if I can't feel her. I believe them, I do – but the problem is that I cannot even feel her mind any more and it makes me think that something really, *really* bad has happened to her.

I am not making any sense, am I?

Maybe I should start from the beginning.

Chapter 2 – Mornings are Always Doomed for Me...

It all started with the Ceremony.

Remember how Mavrose and I had passed the second phase of training as well? With that, we were part of Minecraft and the ranks of their dragon riders. But things still had to be made official! Two days after our big test, I was sleeping in my quarters when Robyn came running in to wake me.

"Steve!"

I groaned and turned over into my bed, burying my face further into my pillows. I was tired and I did not want to be up so early in the morning! In the corner, Mavrose was also fast asleep, little puffs of smoke escaping her huge nostrils as she snored lightly.

"Steve, c'mon!" Robyn shook me. I swatted at her pinching hands and grumbled. I had been up pretty late last night, flying with Mavrose around the village and the forest and I really didn't want to do anything but sleep in!

"Steve, if you don't get up right now, you will regret it!" Robyn growled, frustrated, and I just threw one of my pillows at her before I grabbed another and hid my face with it.

(Yes, I was acting childish... but I was tired!)

With another frustrated grunt, my first friend in Minecraft stomped off and the room fell blessedly silent. Sighing happily into my fluffy pillow, I closed my eyes and breathed out in relief, eager to fall back asleep -

- Only to be awoken rudely when a pail of *icy* cold water was splashed on to my face.

"AAAAAAHHHKKKKK!!!"

I yowled loudly and jumped off my bed, shivering and shrieking. In her corner, Mavrose also jumped up, startled awake and instinctively, she let loose a jet of flame in Robyn's direction.

Baya's rider simply lifted her shield and blocked it like it didn't even matter.

I turned around and glared at her harshly. She was smirking widely, one hand holding her shield and the other gripping at an empty pail.

"What the *heck*, Robyn?" I yelled, rubbing my arms to try and bring sensation back into them. The water was *cold* and my skin was turning numb.

Mavrose rumbled her agreement and slowly shuffled over to where Robyn and I were glaring at one another. She peered down at us with one huge, gem-like eye and snorted.

"I warned you, Steve," Robyn muttered, shrugging. "Not my fault you're an idiot and didn't listen to me."

"Not you-" I sputtered, gritting my teeth. She grinned back at me widely, tossing her hair over her shoulder and patting Mavrose on the snout.

"I know you were up late last night and that you want to rest," she told me, "But the Shahleigh wanna see you. That's why they sent me to wake you up."

My anger vanished and I deflated like a balloon. Well then, that's not something I could grumble about. Hot *dog*.

"You could've just said that instead of drenching me numb," I grumbled sulkily. The light rumble of Mavrose's laughter filled the room and I turned to my dragon, flicking a finger against her scales. Obviously, she didn't even feel it, but it made me feel a bit better.

"Where is the fun in that?" Robyn grinned mischievously. Mavrose leaned down to bump her shoulder with her snout and my friend rubbed her scales affectionately while I continued to sulk and grumble.

(I'd just had ice water dumped on me – *literally*. Can you blame me for a bit of sulking and grumping about?)

A few moments later, Robyn patted my shoulder and turned to go.

"Hurry up and get ready!" she called. "The Shahleigh are expecting you at the pavilion within the hour!"

With that, she stalked off, no doubt in search of her own dragon who was probably waiting for her at the training fields.

Mavrose padded over to me and then bent down, breathing out hot puffs of smoke through her big nostrils. I shivered; it was warm and nice and it made goose bumps rise on my skin after the ice bath I had just had.

"What do you think the Shahleigh want to speak to us about?" I asked her, absent-mindedly rubbing one of her soft wings.

"I am not sure," she answered, "Possibly a quest for us? We have been added to the ranks of the dragon riders here, so I assume it has something to do with that."

I turned to her excitedly.

"Quest?" I exclaimed. "Oh yeah, that is gonna be so cool!"

Being sent on a quest was something I had been dreaming about ever since Mavrose hatched for me. Training is all well and good, but nothing gets your blood pumping like an action filled adventure!

Where would we be sent? I wondered. To an offshore island to rescue a princess trapped there by an evil witch for years together?

Or maybe we would have to go retrieve stolen treasure from a space pirate?

Nervous anticipation bubbled within my belly and I jumped up excitedly, pulling on proper clothes and bustling through my daily routine as quickly as I could. In her corner, Mavrose puffed in amusement, though she didn't say anything.

Suddenly, I couldn't wait to get to the pavilion.

I, Steve, was going to receive my first quest as the Trainer and Rider of an Ender Dragon!

Chapter 3 – My First Quest is a Ceremony...?!

I, Steve, Trainer and Rider of an impressive Ender Dragon did *not* receive my first quest.

It sucked, honestly.

As soon as Mavrose and I were ready, we went over to the breakfast cabin. My dragon padded on ahead while I stopped to quickly grab some fruit to eat at the tables. I followed her out, munching on an apple and savoring the taste of the sweet juice. The early morning air was fresh and crisp and despite the fact that I hadn't gotten much sleep the night before, I was wide awake, enjoying the slight warmth of the rising sun on my skin.

Mavrose was already standing next to the Shahleigh who were waiting for us at the pavilion to the side of the training fields. Out of the corner of my eye, I caught sight of a green flash and I looked up to see Baya diving down from where she had been circling the training grounds in the sky. I waved to my friend and she offered me a friendly growl in acknowledgement before taking off to the sky a second time.

"Good morning, Steve," Tiamat greet me and I smiled at her, swallowing the last of my apple before I bowed low in greeting. I took my place next to Mavrose who dropped her wing over me.

"You wanted to see me?" I asked and Bazr rumbled in agreement.

"We did," Soaban answered. "We have something to tell you."

My heart began beating fast; this was it. This was when I would get my first mission as a dragon rider. This was when I would prove my worth!

"We have something we require of you," Tiamat continued. Before she could say anything else, I jumped in excitedly.

"Yes," I blurted out, "Yes, I'll do it. I'll accept any mission you want me to!"

Mavrose snorted as the Shahleigh fell quietly, watching us confusedly. For a moment, silence prevailed, before it was broken by a low, rumbling sound that I realized was Soaban's laughter.

"Oh, ho, ha-ha," Soaban chuckled. I flushed – why was he laughing!

"Oh young rider," Tiamat sighed and next to her, Bazr breathed out another amused puff of smoke.

"You aren't ready for a mission yet," Soaban said. His voice was not unkind, but I could feel the embarrassment climbing up my neck, as I turned red with indignation.

"Why?" I cried out, "I've completed both phases of my training and I have joined the ranks of the riders! They go out on missions all the time! So why not me?"

I was pouting and I knew it. But they were treating me like a kid! I trained and bonded with an *Ender* Dragon, shouldn't that count for something?

"That's just it, young rider," Tiamat replied. "You haven't joined the ranks of the riders. At least, not yet and not fully."

I stopped short.

"Wait, what?" I sputtered. "I went through all that training – two rounds of it – nearly died a couple of times, and I am not an official rider? Are you kidding me?"

Mavrose growled from next to me. I swatted away her wing and she huffed in annoyance smacking my arm with her snout before turning to the Shahleigh.

"Explain to us, please," her voice was firm but respectful. *Be polite!* She scolded me privately, through the mental link that bound us and I scowled, falling silent nonetheless.

I felt like an idiot. Here I was, running to see what my first mission would be and instead, I was told that I wasn't even an official rider yet!

What a horrid way to start the day.

"You see," Bazr began, "You have completed the main phase of your training. You have earned the right to be part of Minecraft and you have trained and bonded with your Ender Dragon, which is no small feat indeed."

"But," Tiamat took up the narrative; "We do need to officially induct you into our Order of Riders."

"The rest of the trainers haven't met you," it was Soaban's turn, "Nor have they any idea how good you are or how well you perform as Dragon and Rider. Your training may be complete, but you have a long way to get, young rider."

"I'm lost," I shrugged. "What does this mean exactly?"

"It means that we will have an official ceremony to name you as part of our Order," Bazr replied. "The Induction Ceremony will introduce you to all of

Minecraft and you will showcase your skills as Dragon and Rider so that your fellow Trainers will know who you are and what you are capable of."

"Are you willing to do this, Steve, Mavrose?" Tiamat's voice was unusually formal and I scowled at her.

"Do we have a choice?" I muttered. Soaban chuckled again.

"You always have a choice, young rider," he murmured kindly.

I sighed. "Yes," I answered, "We will. Though I am still confused about what we must do, actually..."

Mavrose growled in agreement, tilting her huge head to one side and staring at the Shahleigh with an intensity that would have made anyone else uncomfortable.

"What must we do to prove our mettle as worthy Dragon and Rider?" she asked. Bazr nodded towards the training fields.

"Since you are most familiar with Robyn and Baya, we have asked them to help you get ready," he said. "They will tell you what you must do and how to prepare."

"The Induction Ceremony will take place in three weeks," Soaban added. "At the end of which, you will officially be named as Steve of Minecraft, Rider and Trainer of the Ender Dragon, Mavrose."

"Prepare well, young rider," Tiamat leaned forward; her long, stripy tongue leapt out to lightly lick at my forearm in comfort before she pulled back and padded away, her tail swishing behind her. The other two offered me good-luck nods before they also turned around and followed her out of the pavilion, to wherever they spent their time when not directing things around camp. I sighed and leaned back against Mavrose who puffed out a hot tendril of smoke over my shoulder. The back of my neck prickled as I groaned in annoyance.

"Great," I mumbled, "More training or preparing or whatever."

"Stop grumbling," Mavrose said sternly. "You've been sulking all morning and it is not endearing."

I grunted in response before pulling away. "C'mon," I said, walking off in the direction of the training fields. "Let's go find Robyn and Baya and see what to do about this."

It would, if nothing else, be a hoot.

Chapter 4 – Why is it Always *More* Training?

After our talk with the Shahleigh, Mavrose and I walked back into the training fields in search of Baya and Robyn. The two of them were off in a quiet corner of their own, away from the rest of the crowd, Robyn on Baya's back as the green dragon streaked through the sky, executing complicated maneuvers.

I watched quietly, appreciating the complete ease with which both Baya and Robyn were training. I like to think of myself as quite good with riding a dragon and being comfortable with the quick motions of flight that Mavrose does, but this...this was something on a totally different scale!

For example... Baya was gliding through the air effortlessly, high above the sky. Robyn, without any hesitation whatsoever, just let her hands go. Without even holding on to any part of Baya, she simply stood up in her saddle and balanced on her own two feet, despite the fact that she was flying on a dragon.

My jaw dropped open in utter shock when Baya swerved hard to the right. Robyn, arms open, fell.

"Robyn!" I yelled, my heart hammering in my chest. Next to me, Mavrose was growling, crouched on her hind legs, ready to intervene. The moment she saw Robyn fall, she jumped, taking off into the sky and racing to where my friend was hurtling towards the ground.

But as it turned out, we did not need to worry in the slightest.

Before Mavrose could so much as get close to her, Baya swooped in neatly and flew right below where Robyn was. My human friend, who had been falling to the ground with her arms wide open, now curled up and then rolled over so that she was in perfect position. When Baya swooped in below her, she quickly fell into her saddle in a smooth move, reaching out to wrap her arms around one of the green dragon's spikes, patting her affectionately.

I stumbled back, heaving in relief, my heart still racing a mile a minute. My palms were sweaty and I rubbed them on my breeches to get rid of the icky feeling as I waited for my friends to land.

Baya landed first, Robyn clambering off her with a wide grin on her face. As she got off, she reached out to press a quick kiss to her dragon's snout before she turned to me with the same happy smile.

I, on the other hand, was not amused. I marched up to her, glaring at her.

"What in the world was that, Robyn?" I yelled. Mavrose landed just then, padding over to us, her entire body vibrating with a growing rumble of concern.

Robyn blinked. "Wasn't that brilliant?" she exclaimed enthusiastically, "*Man*, it was an exhilarating feeling!"

I was still breathing heavily, relief and annoyance warring within me.

"I thought you were gonna get hurt, Robyn!" I protested and her gaze softened. She reached out to ruffle my hair and I swatted at her hand indignantly.

"Steve," she sighed, "You're an idiot."

"Hey!"

"While I agree with that statement, Robyn," Mavrose interjected and I turned my glare on my dragon, "That was a bit dangerous, don't you think?"

Baya chuckled softly and padded over to us, bumping my shoulder with a friendly snout.

"Do you truly think I would let my human get hurt, Steve?" she asked softly. Her voice was amused, not irritated, and I flushed.

"I-I guess...not," I stuttered. "But..."

Robyn chuckled and leaned over to hug me.

"You're a good friend, Steve," she said warmly. "But this is also part of training. As dragon and rider, you are meant for the skies."

She looked upward, gaze faraway.

"The freedom, the fall... it's absolutely *exhilarating*!"

She looked at me with a wide smile. "You'll have to do that, you know... for your Induction Ceremony."

"WHAT?" I yelped, eyes going wide. "I have to – what?"

Baya licked my shoulder with the tip of a barbed tongue and I swatted at her instinctively.

"Indeed, Steve," she said amusedly. "What did you think you were going to be doing?"

"That...sounds... well, interesting," Mavrose said slowly. I grunted and turned to her in frustration.

"Have you lost your mind, Mavrose?" I scowled. "I'm not jumping off you like *that*."

One huge, gemstone eye opened to stare me chillingly. I held back a flinch. If you have never been on the receiving end of an Ender Dragon's glare, let me tell you – it's scary.

"Don't you trust me to catch you?" she growled. Next to us, Baya and Robyn fell silent, watching curiously but not intervening. "Was not the whole point of our training learning to trust in one another? Have I not earned your faith, human?!"

I felt the undercurrent of hurt from her lighting up the back of my mind and I squirmed. I hated it when she did that.

Sighing, I held out my hand and she licked it, eyes narrowing.

"I trust you," I mumbled. "But..."

I looked up at the sky again. It wasn't that I was scared exactly... I did trust Mavrose. We have been through a lot together and I *know* she won't let me get hurt. It's just...

The idea of it all... it was so *big*! An Induction Ceremony was a big thing. I was going to be introduced to *everyone*. I would meet all the riders and trainers, who were all a hundred times more experienced than me, who all had bonded to their dragons well before I had and who were powerful and strong and went on amazing missions at the drop of a hat.

Who was *I*, to compete with all that?

Just little Steve, school kid who couldn't even save himself from bullies.

"It's overwhelming, isn't it?" Robyn spoke up. Her voice was quiet and I nodded.

"Yeah, it is," I replied.

For a moment, we were silent. Then I grunted with resolve, squared my shoulders and turned to her.

"I am going to do this and I am going to get it right," I told her determinedly. "Help me?"

Baya snorted and dropped a wing over me. Mavrose growled in a low tone before reaching out with her tail and then entangling it with the green dragon's.

"Of course," Robyn hugged me. "Let's begin then!"

And so we started yet another round of training.

Chapter 5 – Split Second Timing, My Foot.

Training *sucked*.

For one, I was still annoyed that I had to get through yet another phase of training before I could start going on missions with my dragon. Wasn't *two* rounds enough?! But this time at least, it wasn't serious or painful – just a lot of hard work and practice.

Oh and the whole lot of bruising and pain I was in, but hey what's a little ache compared to being made a fool out of in front of all my would-be peers?

To be honest though, training was also kind of fun. Baya explained the whole Ceremony to us very quickly and told us what we would have to do.

"First," she began, "You must bathe in the river before you dress in ceremonial clothing. The waters of the river will serve to purify your body and spirit. After that, you will prove your worth as dragon rider in the training arena."

"The maneuver you just saw me do?" Robyn continued where her dragon left off. "That's one of the many things you'll have to do. A series of exercises to prove just how good a rider you are – after that, you will be expected to battle one of the other riders in the arena."

"I have to – what?!" I sputtered. "I don't even know how to fight, Robyn!"

She rolled her eyes.

"What do you think Baya and I are going to teach you, stupid?" she punched my arm and I winced – the girl had a mean right hook.

"And win or lose, it doesn't matter," Baya said wisely, "It is simply to prove your strength as a rider. The Shahleigh would like for you to showcase your skills to the others... many wonder if you are worthy of a dragon, particularly one like Mavrose."

She cast a meaningful look at my dragon who snorted out an amused puff of smoke.

"Indeed," my dragon's eyes glinted with amusement, "No one would expect a runt like you for an Ender Dragon's trainer."

I huffed, glaring at her.

"Stop mocking me," I grumbled and she chuckled, the tip of her tongue darting out to lick my ear before she moved back. I grunted and then hugged her snout.

"So what are we starting with?" I asked Robyn, who pointed to where she had set up a bunch of pillows and bedding on the ground.

"When you did your physical training with Mavrose," she stated, "You focused on building up endurance and strength, am I correct?"

I blinked, thrown at the reference to my own training. "Uh, yeah," I nodded, the memory resurfacing. Man, it felt like such a long time ago now, even though it's been barely a month!

"We need to work on your speed and your timing then," Robyn said. "Strength is important as is physical endurance, but agility is equally necessary.

You and Mavrose need to work on getting your timing exactly right."

"In the skies, there is no room for mistakes," Baya said gravely, "If you miss a landing, or you are not able to match Mavrose's movements, you will plunge to a painful death."

"I won't let him fall so easily," Mavrose growled. Baya snorted.

"In the heat of battle," she said kindly, "You cannot be distracted. You cannot afford to worry about protecting your human when you are fighting off a foe."

Mavrose subsided and I stroked the under tip of her wing in comfort. I needed to learn these things – we would be the stronger as dragon and rider for it.

So we began. Robyn made me climb to the top of the roof and then jump off, plummeting to the ground as Mavrose swooped in to try and catch me.

She failed.

Six times!

Six times, I fell to the bedding and rolled over, groaning as my entire body ached.

My dragon was utterly frustrated – she kept growling in displeasure and snorting out puffs of smoke that were soon turning into tiny jets of flame. Any more and she would soon be roaring in anger and letting loose full streams of fire at unsuspecting victims.

I was just as exasperated.

We trusted each other, we had trained together and still, *why* were we having so much difficulty?!

It was driving me insane.

Each time, I would jump off the roof, tensed and arms flailing about, grappling for purchase, waiting for my dragon to rescue me. And each time, her timing would be off by just a second or two, swooping in as I hit the mattress on the floor with a loud thud.

(Word to the wise – *don't* try this at home! It's painful and makes you bruise all over!)

Finally, after almost three hours of this kind of torture, Baya and Robyn called for a halt.

"That's enough," Robyn held out a hand for me and I grabbed it, yanking myself up from where I lay on the bedding. I was black and blue all over and every part of my body ached.

"What am I doing wrong?!" I threw up my hands in frustration. Next to me Mavrose growled loudly.

"*You* are doing nothing wrong," Robyn responded. I huffed, whirling to Baya.

"Then what is she doing wrong?" I jabbed a finger in Mavrose's direction. Next thing I knew, I was yelping in surprise as I was thrown into the ground again, this time pushed down by an indignant Ender Dragon's snout.

"I am not doing anything wrong, human," Mavrose roared. I groaned and just stood up on shaky legs, ignoring her and focusing on Baya.

"Mavrose is right," the green dragon agreed, "*she* is doing nothing wrong."

I blinked.

"Then why can't we get this right?!" I exclaimed, utterly exasperated by now. Today was not going well at all.

"Because both of you are working as two distinct units, Steve," Robyn answered softly. "As dragon and rider, you need to work together. You said that you trust Mavrose. Then prove it."

I froze, eyes widening in shock.

"Wh-what?"

"You must learn to anticipate each other's movements," Baya replied. "The emotional bond that you share must translate itself into a physical one as well... you will need to learn to treat Mavrose's wings as an extension of your own self and trust that she will not let you fall."

It was something to consider.

Truly, I trusted my dragon. And I trusted that she wouldn't let me fall or let me get hurt. But I had never really considered flying as something I could do. As a rider, it was Mavrose who did the moving and the maneuvering – I was just along for the ride, even if I was the one who trained her.

God, I am stupid sometimes.

Yes, you are. Mavrose, who had apparently been listening in on my inner monologue with myself, sounded smug. I bumped her with my shoulder and scowled at her.

"Can we try again?" I asked Robyn. My friend shook her head.

"Not today," she answered. "You need to rest up and the Shahleigh wanted to meet with me and Baya after training was done for the day. Let's go grab some food. I need my strength for that."

"Is everything alright?" I asked her as we began the trek back to the dining area. She didn't reply for a long moment and I squeezed her shoulder.

"Robyn?" I called, "Is everything alright?"

She shook herself and turned to me with a wide smile.

"Nothing, Steve," she responded, refusing to meet my eyes. "Everything is fine, don't worry. I'm just hungry."

With that, she bounded on ahead, Baya following her quietly.

Something is not right, Mavrose said quietly. She didn't speak out loud, which meant that she too had sensed the uneasiness within our friends. A worried look passed between us before we also followed the two of them into the dining area to eat.

Yeah, I replied. *But...*

We'll just have to keep our eyes open.

Yeah, I agreed with a sigh.

Go eat, silly human, she pushed me on with her snout. *It will all work out eventually.*

If only she knew then how wrong she was...

Chapter 6 – A Secret Revealed

The next couple of days followed the same pattern. Mavrose and I would wake up early in the morning, head to the dining area where we would have a very light breakfast.

(Eat something heavy and the next thing you know, you're throwing up from all the swerving around in the sky. I learnt that the hard way.)

After eating, Robyn and Baya would take us to their little corner of the training arena, where the former would pad up the ground and the latter would take Mavrose aside to instruct on her more complicated flying maneuvers.

The first half of the day was individual training; Mavrose and Baya took to the skies, with the green dragon leading my own in flight. It was when I was watching them that I realized the truth of what the Shahleigh had told me a while back.

Ender dragons are fierce and proud, they had told me, *who love the freedom of the skies more than anything else.*

Watching Mavrose naturally race through all the tasks Baya put her through made me realize just how much my black dragon loved to fly. I could feel her delight light up the back of my mind and it made me smile.

My own training with Robyn, however, was not easy. In fact, it was the downright hardest thing I have ever had to do!

She was teaching me how to fight with swords. To practice with, we had these wooden sticks that would serve as weapons until she deemed me ready to battle with an actual sword. Needless to say, I was nowhere near that at the moment.

The first session went something like this. I took the wooden sword in my hand and tried to spin it around, feeling confident and like a superhero.

The stupid thing fell to the ground with a loud thud and when I went to pick it up, Robyn attacked me from behind, hitting me with her stick and then bringing me to my knees with a well aimed swerve of her right leg.

"Never take your eyes off the enemy, Steve," she smirked, standing over me, her features arranged in a look of pride and victory. I groaned and then pushed her off of me, jumping up, ready to retaliate –

- only to be defeated and thrown back on my butt barely a few minutes later. The girl is a veritable fighter with the instincts of a soldier.

No wonder I didn't have a single chance.

But I didn't give up. I worked hard and under her tutelage, the stupid wooden sword was turning from a useless piece of junk I was bandying about to a powerful tool that would serve as my defense in dire need.

After my sword fighting lesson, we would have a quick lunch, against some light fare, following which came the maneuver lessons. And these were not easy, let me tell you! More often than not, Mavrose and I missed each other – our timing was *always* a split second off and by the time Robyn called it quits for the day, I was black, blue and purple all over from falling off the roof repeatedly.

But neither Mavrose nor I had the energy or the time to complain about how exhausting this schedule was.

Because something was going on, something serious that had both Robyn and Baya worried. There was a strange sort of unease in the air – both of them would space out randomly or share these strange looks. I knew they could talk to one another mentally the way Mavrose and I could, and I longed to know what they were discussing that was so secret.

I was being nosy, but whatever it was, it was deeply worrying them and both Mavrose and I could see it. I wanted to confront Robyn and ask her about it, but my dragon talked me out of that plan – she knew Baya well enough to know that the green dragon would not easily give up her secrets.

"We must wait until they are ready to share with us, Steve," she had puffed irritatedly when I told her again that we needed to just demand to know what was going on.

I snorted in disbelief, "Yeah, when? After something major happens and they end up hurt?"

"I am as frustrated as you are, human," Mavrose had snapped, a small jet of flame streaking towards me. I yelped and ducked; a second later, the fire sailed past my head and I glared up at my grumpy dragon who glared right back at me. a moment later, I dropped my gaze and flushed in embarrassment.

"Sorry," I muttered and Mavrose huffed.

"I worry about them too," she said after a moment's silence and I sighed, leaning back against her and wishing I knew when my life began to spin so out of control.

The conversation came back to me a week later when Mavrose and I were training with Robyn and Baya again. Only this time, neither of my friends was interested in working with us and it was obvious.

Robyn was utterly distracted – she kept missing her swerves and I was easily able to get away from her sword. A part of me wanted to believe that it was because I had gotten better at fighting, but I knew that that wasn't the case.

With a loud yell, I swung my wooden sword into her left side; she sidestepped me, but then tripped on the leg I held out and went down with a startled shriek. Before she could roll over and pick up her fallen sword, I grabbed it and held it to her chest in a sign of obvious victory.

She stared up at me in startled wonder, as if pondering how silly old me – school kid with no experience whatsoever – just defeated her. I huffed and held out my hand for her to grab, jerking my head in the direction of our dragons who were watching us quietly.

"You- how-how...what?" she stuttered as I pulled her to her feet. We walked over to where Baya and Mavrose were lying on the ground, having completed their flight practice for the day already.

"You and I both know that I am not near good enough to beat you," I told her firmly as I sat down next to Mavrose. I was sweating and so was Robyn and she handed me a bottle of water, which I gulped at thirstily.

"Steve," Mavrose rumbled a warning but I shook my head. This had gone on long enough.

"Tell me what's wrong, Robyn," I demanded. "You're so distracted that even a dumb novice like me could beat you. What is going on?"

"Noth-" Baya began and I glared at her, cutting her off.

"Don't say nothing," I snapped. "You're distracted and you won't even talk to us outside of training. What is happening?"

They both fell silent, sharing a secret look, communicating silently.

"We want to help you," Mavrose added. The element of sincerity in her usually pompous and grumpy tone must have surprised them; Baya stared us for a long moment before she sighed and then nodded at Robyn, who plopped down next to her with a long groan.

"Okay fine," she muttered. "I'll tell you, but you must promise not to tell anyone, okay?!"

I nodded, "Of course. I promise."

"Mavrose?" Robyn peered up at my dragon expectantly. The easy camaraderie between them made me smile; it seems like ages ago when Robyn was so taken by the idea of an Ender Dragon that she just stared up at Mavrose in awe. Now, she treats her like a normal friend and it never fails to put a smile on my face.

"I give you my word, Robyn, Baya," Mavrose swore solemnly.

"Now spill," I said impatiently.

"I-I..." Robyn looked uncharacteristically nervous.

"Go on," I encouraged her, "You what-?"

"I'm going on a mission!" she blurted out. "The Shahleigh have given me a difficult one and I am leaving next week."

I froze. A quest? Robyn was going on...a quest?

Wait, did she say *next week?*

"Wh-what?!" I sputtered. "Say that again?!"

"Remember when I said that I had a meeting with them?" she said, "That was actually a debriefing. Baya and I are going on a secret quest and we have been preparing for it... that's why I've been spacing out so much."

Jealousy reared up within me; *I* wanted to go to. Whatever this quest was, it was important. I was a rider and a trainer, to an Ender Dragon no less, and I wanted the adventure that Robyn was getting.

"Uh...well, I uh..." I didn't know what to say.

"You leave a week from now?" Mavrose asked. Baya bumped her with her snout.

"Yes," the green dragon rumbled softly. "We are sorry we cannot help you with training, but we will return before the Ceremony begins. That's why we've been pushing you so hard these past few days."

"You'll have to train by yourself for the next week or so," Robyn told me. "I was gonna tell you before I left, but... I guess I didn't know how... I know you wanted a quest of your own and...." She trailed off, uncertain and worried.

I felt like an idiot at that point. Yes, I wanted a quest and I wanted to be acknowledged as a rider and trainer, but that didn't mean I didn't want my friend to be happy! Robyn was an awesome fighter and I knew she was going to do great!

Reaching out, I hugged her tightly.

"Hey, it's fine," I murmured. "You go on your quest and kick butt, okay? I'll be fine... we can manage for a couple of days without you."

I pulled back with a grin and Robyn smiled back happily before she turned to my black dragon.

"Mavrose, I-" she stammered. Baya's tail swished nervously but she remained silent.

"Steve is right," Mavrose interrupoted. "It is of no consequence. Go on your quest and return safely. We shall be fine."

Robyn, looking relieved, hugged my dragon's snout. I ran my hand down the side of Baya's scales and she dropped a wing over me, licking the tip of my hand with her long tongue.

"Thank you, Steve," she rumbled. I smiled.

"Yeah," I answered. "You guys are gonna do great!"

My optimism, as it would turn out, was completely displaced.

Three days after we had that conversation with Baya and Robyn, the two of them left on their quest. They came to see us in the morning before they left. Robyn woke me up that morning and I saw her off with as much energy as I could muster despite the jealousy that was bubbling in my stomach.

"You're gonna do great," I told her when I pulled back. She was biting her lip nervously and shook her head.

"I wish..." she sighed and I bumped shoulders with her.

"What is it?" I asked softly. She looked at me with a strange expression on her face.

"I wish...I wish you could come too!" she blurted out and then looked away, embarrassed. I stared at her in surprise – how did she know exactly what I had been thinking?!

"Go on, human," Mavrose nudged her gently with her big snout. "It will not be long before we can all undertake a quest together. For now, you must do this by yourself, until we can join you."

Baya leaned in to lick my cheek affectionately before rumbling her agreement.

"Mavrose is right," I told Robyn. "I am super jealous of you, but I know I'll be joining you soon. So go on and kick some major butt for me, okay?! You are going to be awesome!"

She hadn't told me what her quest was supposed to be and I hadn't asked. Each quest that was given to a rider was a secret between them and the Shahleigh, who would allot quests based on the rider's abilities as an individual. Until they returned from it, none of us would know what they had been sent to do. If they came back victorious, then a feast would be held in their honor and they would be allowed to recount the entire adventure.

I was already looking forward to doing that with Robyn and Baya.

"Good luck!" I stepped back as my friend jumped on to her dragon. A moment later, Baya kicked off of her powerful hind legs and then, they were in the sky, leaving me and Mavrose to stare after them worriedly.

"I hope they will be alright," I murmured, still waving at the horizon, where my friends were no larger than a dot.

Mavrose puffed in acknowledgement.

"You worry too much, human," she growled and then turned, padding back to the dining arena to get some breakfast. Her long tail swished after her and I sighed.

She wasn't fooling me with her nonchalance.

I wasn't the only one who was worried.

Chapter 7 – I Learn How *Not* to Punch an Idiot in the Face

With Robyn and Baya gone, Mavrose and I upped our training sessions. We had less than two weeks to get ready for the Induction Ceremony and we needed to be prepared! And that was how we met Fergus and his dragon, Ferdinand.

Given that I was still nowhere close proficient with a sword, I needed proper instruction. I didn't want to make a fool out of myself in front of the whole of Minecraft! So the Shahleigh assigned Fergus to me, to help me practice my sword fighting skills in Robyn's place until she returned.

I didn't like Fergus even half as much as I like Robyn. He was a *moron*.

"Well, well, well, Steve," he smirked as he walked into our training arena. "What an honor it is to instruct the mighty trainer of an Ender Dragon! Are you certain you need my help at all?"

I gritted my teeth; for some reason, I found him irritating. Before I could say anything, he just walked up to Mavrose and leaned in close, flicking the skin between her eyes with his fingers.

She yelped, roaring in pain as she jerked back. The space between a dragon's eyes is extremely sensitive – the skin there is soft, the scales not as hard as the rest of their bodies. It is one of the few vulnerable parts of a dragon's hard body.

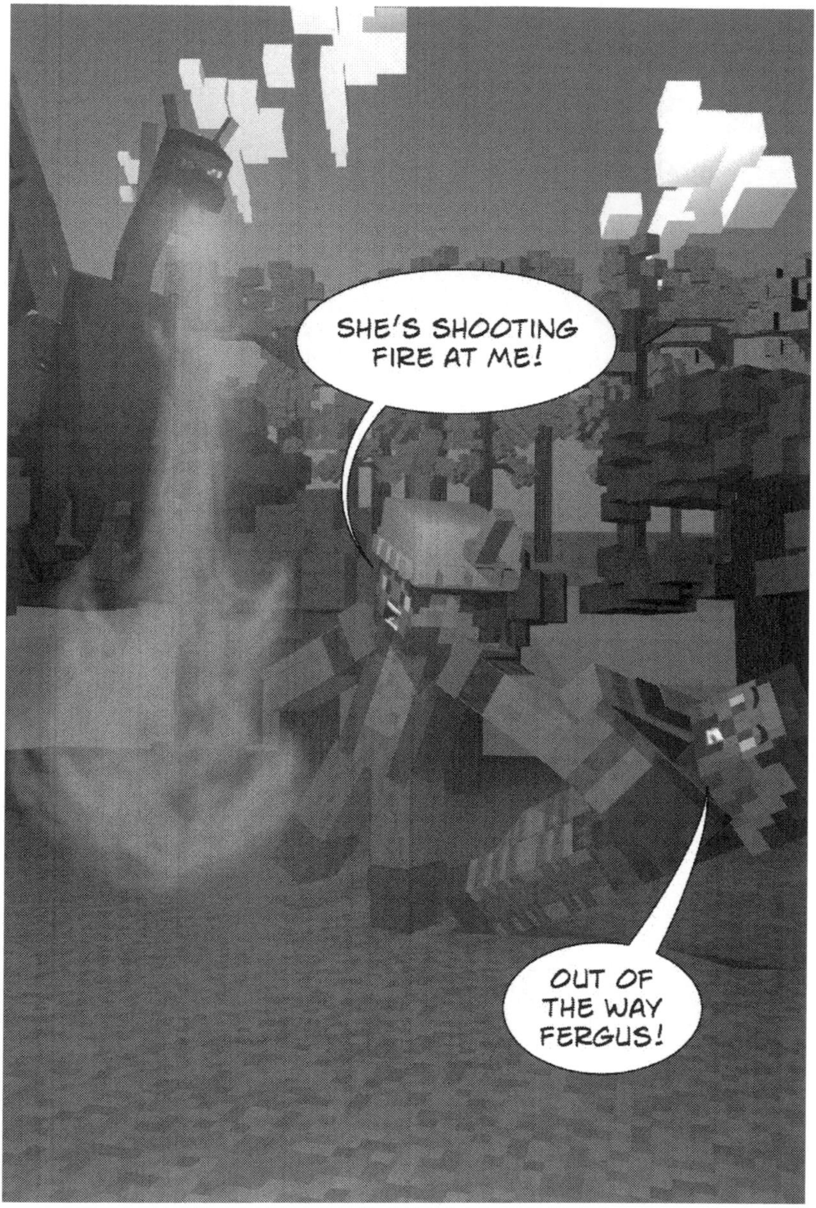
SHE'S SHOOTING FIRE AT ME!
OUT OF THE WAY FERGUS!

"What are you *DOING*?!" I yelled at him, pulling him back. And just in time too.

Ender Dragons are not known for their patience or their forbearance. Mavrose, in a fit of annoyance, let loose a thick, blame jet of flame at Fergus, who ducked and then turned to glare at me.

"Is she mad?" he asked furiously. "She could have *killed* me!"

Behind him, his dragon – a puny little thing with sickly yellow colored scaled that made it look more jaundiced than majestic – growled. It sounded pitiful to me, given that I spent most of my time dealing with Mavrose's extreme grumpiness and loud growls that sound more like thunder than anything else.

"You flicked her eyes, you idiot!" I snapped. "What did you think, that she was going to lick your face in thank you?"

"Watch yourself, human," Mavrose snarled at him and Fergus raised an eyebrow at her.

"I'm here to train you two," he said haughtily. "You are better off showing me the respect I deserve."

Mavrose growled low in her throat, opening her jaws to let loose another jet of flame. I jumped in front of her in a preemptive strike, shaking my head when she puffed in frustration.

"Steve," she snarled in warning, "You-"

"Mavrose, we have less than two weeks left," I snapped at her. "We can't afford to antagonize him."

We really don't have a choice until Robyn and Baya get back, I told her silently. *All the other trainers are either busy with their own quests or don't want to work with us...*

Because they're afraid of an Ender Dragon? She sounded scornful. *Cowards. They are right to fear me. I have no use for the weak willed.*

Whatever it is, we really don't have a choice but to train with him, so snap out of it!

She growled again, but subsided. Fergus, who had been watching us with a slight smirk, clapped his hands delightedly.

"Wonderful, then!" he said. "Let's begin!"

For all that he was an annoying gnat (Mavrose's words, not mine), the guy knew how to fight. He was as good as Robyn was – he threw me on my butt flat within ten minutes.

"Steve," he chortled as he stood over me in victory. "Are you sure Mavrose is yours? How *ever* did you manage to train an Ender Dragon when you can't even defeat little old me in a simple match of swords?"

I gritted my teeth, breathing out slowly. He was a bully, just like all those bullies from my school I had once run away from. I wasn't going to let him get to me, not this time.

I insisted on finishing my training with him, completing my routine as scheduled. By the end of it, I was sick of his running commentary and taunting that I just wanted to let Mavrose roast him to a pulp like I knew she wanted to do.

Just a few more days, I reminded myself. *Baya and Robyn will be back soon, and I will never have to see his smug face again.*

And may that day come soon, Mavrose yowled into my mind, grumpy. *I do not like him or his silly dragon. Ferdinand looks like a fly could swat him. And he is supposed to help me with my flight? I would teach that young whelp a thing or two about the sky.*

I chuckled, leaning back into her. We were back in our quarters, training done for the day and I curled up with her in her corner. I liked to do this occasionally, instead of sleeping on my own bed, especially on cold days. A dragon is always warm – they have literal fires in their bellies that keep their skin nice and hot to touch. So when she dropped a wing around me and drew me closer to the underside of her belly, I sighed in delight.

I was warm, safe and drowsy. It didn't take long for me fall asleep.

This trend continued for the next week. and let me tell you, it is a true testament to my patience that I did not end up punching Fergus over the course of the time we trained together.

He is an arrogant, smug, irritating idiot who thinks he is better than everyone else! It took all I had to ignore him; I really, really wanted to kick his butt, not because I liked fighting, but because I didn't like anyone treating me badly.

I stopped short at the thought. Huh... I guess coming to Minecraft, bonding with and training with a grumpy, super powerful dragon had taught me to stand up for myself!

But that's no excuse to indulge in mindless violence, so I sighed and just focused all my energy into beating him during our sword matches. I was still a novice, so that idea didn't go all that well! But I tried and slowly, each day, I improved bit by bit. My dragon, on the other hand, had just flat out refused to work with Ferdinand.

I have to admit, she is a hundred times better at flying and maneuvering than that yellow runt anyway, so I couldn't really protest.

But we were both getting worried about Robyn and Baya. They were supposed to have returned by now and we had heard no word from them. The Induction Ceremony was only a few days away and neither of us wanted to go through it without them there.

And then, less than a week before the Ceremony, things went mad.

Chapter 8 – Fire in the Hole!

Both Mavrose and I were fast asleep in our quarters when Tiamat burst in, growling loudly.

"Steve!" she snarled, "Wake your dragon now!"

I startled awake and behind me, Mavrose exhaled in a rush, a hot puff of smoke escaping her nostrils as she reared up, peering to see what was going on.

"On your feet now, young rider!"

I had never heard Tiamat sound so worried or flustered. I knew something was wrong right away and I scrambled up, jumping on to Mavrose, whose tail was swishing back and forth in agitation.

"What's going on?" I yelled over the wind as we took to the skies, following the Shahleigh.

"Robyn and Baya are in dire need of help!" Tiamat answered. My face became pale and my heart began to hammer a mile a minute as fear bubbled like acid in my stomach.

In all my excitement about adventure, I'd forgotten one little detail – quests could be *dangerous*.

And clearly, my friends were in the middle of that danger.

Mavrose needed no urging from me to speed up; her wings flapped with a sense of righteous fury as we followed Tiamat through the skies, flying high over Minecraft to where I supposed Robyn and Baya were.

It didn't take us long to reach the place.

The night air in Minecraft is generally quite cold; as we flew through the velvet sky, I could see my breath in front of me as it crusted over and then vanished into the ether.

I felt the heat before I saw the fire. Suddenly, it was very, *very* warm, the air smelling acrid with a familiar stink – smoke.

As a dragon rider, I was well acquainted with the smell of smoke.

My hands were suddenly sweating and as Tiamat dived down, I knew – without her saying anything – what we were going to find.

The hut was ablaze, the fire rising up in powerful columns of orange and yellow, dancing and licking its way along the sides of the little firmament. I could hear the screams of the villagers down on the ground

– it sent a shiver down my spine and I hoped desperately that nobody was stuck inside.

Robyn and Baya... what if they were stuck inside?!

Terror clogged my throat, but I leaned forward in my saddle and mentally urged Mavrose to go faster. In moments, we were landing in front of the fire and she was shaking me off. I stumbled to the ground, clambering off her with shaky legs. Before I could say anything, she jumped again, taking off in the direction of the hut.

"NOOO!" I shrieked, "Mavrose, come back!"

"Fire will not harm me!" she shouted back as she flapped her wings furiously. "Not as much as it will harm you! I am an *Ender* Dragon, these flames will *not* defeat me!"

She vanished into the smoke and I could only watch helplessly. Before I could do something stupid like break down and cry, the villagers were surrounding me, pushing pails of water into my hands and begging me to help them.

I joined them, throwing water over the fire and filling up pail after pail with trembling hands. The fire was slowly quenching down, but I didn't know where Mavrose, Baya or Robyn were and I was terrified.

Just then, a loud yowl pierced through the air.

"Mavrose!" I yelled for my dragon, dropping the pail I was holding. My heart was racing and my hands were clammy with sweat, but I didn't care.

I turned around, watching the fire expectantly.

From the smoke, a huge, bulky dragon-esque figure emerged. I squinted, trying to get a glimpse of who it could be – in the bright yellow flames, I couldn't differentiate between the dark green of Baya's scales from the sheer black of Mavrose's.

Mavrose, c'mon! I sent out impatiently.

There was no response. I hadn't seen Tiamat in a while either and I was shaking hard, fear and anxiety crawling beneath my skin.

The figure emerged, coughing and snarling and yowling. She collapsed on the ground in front of us, breathing heavily, the bright sheen of a dragon's scales reduced to a dull shine in the wake of the black soot and dust that covered.

The scales were green.

It was Baya, not Mavrose.

And Robyn was nowhere to be seen.

I yelled in surprise and ran to her, calling out for Mavrose even as I hugged Baya's snout.

"Mavrose?!" I cried out again and again. "Mavrose, answer me! Robyn? Mavrose?!"

There was no response. So I reached out with my mind, trying to call her mentally –

- only to be met with silence, because none of my cries were getting through to my dragon, whom I could no longer feel.

MAVROSE!

I was no longer connected to my dragon.

Chapter 9 – A Waiting Game...

The fire was one of the worst catastrophes to hit the village in almost a decade. Or so the villagers told me as I waited outside the Healers' huts after I helped carry Baya inside.

Once it was put out, I ran into the remaining soot covered, tattered hut to see if Robyn or Mavrose were still there. I knew that it was a silly hope, but I needed to see for myself. Obviously, there was nothing there but charred wood.

None of the villagers had been hurt, thankfully.

But Baya was injured pretty badly and Tiamat insisted that she not be disturbed until she was healed.

And so, now I am left waiting for her to awaken so that we can question her about what had happened. The Shahleigh are refusing to tell me about the quest that they sent my friends on and so far, I haven't had the energy to argue with them.

I didn't realize how much I depended on my bond with Mavrose until it was gone. Not being able to hear her grumpy, sarcastic voice in my mind is driving me insane, which is why I sat down to write all of this , as a way to distract myself. I am so, so worried for her! We didn't find anything in the hut to indicate that she or Robyn had been hurt, but I don't know where she is... I want her back so badly!

I will have to wait for Baya to wake up so that I can find just what happened inside. I don't care what the Shahleigh say about quest propriety; I am getting my dragon back, even if I have to force Baya to tell me all about it!

The Induction Ceremony is less than a week away and there is no way I am letting my dragon miss it. She is a force unto herself and the whole of Minecraft will see it!

I am coming, Mavrose, just hang in there!

To be Continued in How To Train Your Ender Dragon 4 – Enemy Kin!

Special Free Comics Offer From Funny Comics

Funny Comics is the leading publisher of funny stories, comics and graphic novels on the web. Make sure to "LIKE" our fan page on Facebook below:

https://www.facebook.com/FunnyComics3000

On this page we will share news on everything we are up to as well as notify you when our comics are available for FREE on Kindle.

Other Comics And Short Stories From Funny Comics

The DIARY OF A FRIENDLY CREEPER Series

In this illustrated short story series the Friendly Creeper is a bit of an outcast. Despite the fact that he is creeper he doesn't share his brethren's desire to scare people. All he wants to do is make friends! Follow his journey as he tries to show that there can be more to creepers than being scary!

How To Train Your Ender Dragon Series

In this series of illustrated short stories Steve Montgomery is your typical 15 year old kid with 15 year old problems. However, there is one unusual thing about him. Steve Montgomery has the power to summon dragons ...

Minecraft: How To Train Your Ender Dragon

Steve Montgomery is your typical 15 year old with 15 year old problems. The biggest of which is that he is often bullied by a group of kids that includes his own brother. Steve has something that most other kids don't have, however, for he has the power to summon dragons. After he is literally strung up a flagpole by his tormentors Steve meets a magical dragon who not only saves him but whisks him away to the magical world of Minecraft. However once he arrives there he soon learns that other dangers exist besides school bullies. ...

The Adventures Of Fartman Series

In this series of illustrated short stories you will thrill to the adventures of Minecraft's greatest hero, Fartman! Armed only with the power of his farts read along as Fartman works to protect his home and friends from the schemes of the evil Enderman!

The Adventures Of Fartman – The Beginning

Steve has a problem. He farts. He farts like no one has ever farted. He farts so badly that it's hard for him to make friends or even hold a job. However when the village he lives in is threatened by the nefarious Enderman Steve starts to see his farting curse as a potential gift. Read this story and witness as he transforms himself from mild mannered Steve into the mighty Fart Man!

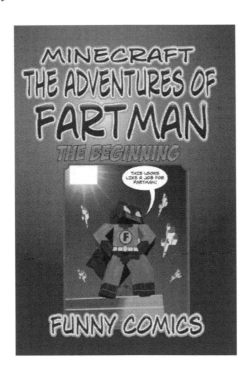

Diary Of A Misunderstood Herobrine Series

In this series of illustrated short stories you will get to experience life from Herobrine's point of view. Is Herobrine really bad, or just misunderstood?

Diary Of A Misunderstood Herobrine: It Ain't Easy Being Mean

Everyone knows Herobrine is the villain in Minecraft, but was it always this way? What's more, how did Herobrine get this way to begin with? In this illustrated short story Herobrine tells all from his perspective. At first he really only wanted to build things and help people. However, everyone he meets just won't accept him at his word. Maybe being a bad guy isn't that bad after all?

The MINECRAFT STEVE ADVENTURES Series

In this comic series Steve must use the power of his imagination in order to defeat the evil plans of Herobrine. We've based stories so far on Jurassic Park, Star Wars and The Wizard Of Oz. More to come!

Minecraft Steve Adventures: Jurassic Block

Minecraft Steve Adventures: Attack On The Death Square

Minecraft Steve Adventures: Frozen – Baby It's Cold Outisde

Minecraft Steve Adventures: That's How You Get Ants, Man!

Minecraft Steve Adventures – The Craving Games

In this illustrated short story Minecraft Steve must use his knowledge of the Hunger Games to defeat Herorbine!

The Adventures Of Big Buddy And Little Buddy Series

In this comic series Big Buddy and Little Buddy are friends, inventors and adventurers. Big Buddy tends to be more serious and practical. Little Buddy? Let's just say a little less so. Nonetheless they always have each others back no matter what trouble they get into!

The Adventures Of Big Buddy And Little Buddy – Escape From Planet X

Reviewers and Friends of Funny Comics Hall of FAME – We LOVE YOU!

As a small, independent publisher we are EXTREMELY appreciative of our fans. The people listed below have either consistently reviewed our books and comics on Amazon or have offered us story ideas / comments to us through the e-mail listed below. This is fantastic as it helps us make our stories better. . We REALLY appreciate your reviews, thoughts and ideas. If you feel like you should be featured in our honor roll below please contact us via our e-mail address. In the meantime here is a list of the people who have really supported us in the past. THANK-YOU ONE AND ALL!

W. Shi – New York City

Stephanie Linn

May Ong – Singapore

Patrick Jane – Orlando

Lin

Dude89 (via Patricia G. ;))

WD

Hannah

Funnycomics1@gmail.com

Thank-you again for reading our story and we hope you enjoyed it!

Made in the USA
San Bernardino, CA
11 September 2017